The Challah That Took Over the House

* * *

Melissa Berg

Illustration by
Shiela Marie

Eclectic Ivri Press

http://www.eclecticivripress.com

Publisher's Note: This is a work of fiction. Names, characters, places, and incidents are a product of the author's imagination. Locales and public names are sometimes used for atmospheric purposes. Any resemblance to actual people, living or dead, or to businesses, companies, events, institutions, or locales is completely coincidental.

Ordering Information: Special discounts are available on quantity purchases by corporations, associations, and others. For details, contact the publisher at the address above.

Eclectic Ivri Press. — First Edition

ISBN 978-0-9921637-5-4
Printed in the United States of America

For my Bubbie, Yetta

1

Challah in the House

"But you promised! If I don't like it here, I can move back to Golders Green and stay with Auntie Aviva."

Raizy was trying one more argument. She did NOT under any circumstances, want to remain on Sunnyside Avenue even ONE MORE DAY. The building that she now lived in housed three other girls. They were not the least bit friendly.

"Raizy! You're going to be late for school," Raizy's mom yelled.

"But Mom!" Raizy picked up her backpack and stomped out the door.

It was Friday. There was only a half day of class. Each girl came home with her own personal challah dough to bake. Their parents would help them when they returned from work.

Maya passed Sheva. She whispered, "My challah will be better than yours. It's sweet."

When Atara passed Maya in the hallway, she yelled, "My challah will be better than yours. It's saucy."

Sheva yelled back, "My challah will be better than yours. It's spicy."

When Raizy passed Atara, she yelled, "My challah will be better than yours. It's super chocolaty."

Maya passed Raizy and noticed her chocolate chip dough. Maya raised one eyebrow.

"What?" Raizy yelled.

"Chocolate, it's for cake. Not challah."

Uggggh … Raizy hated them all.

Raizy entered her apartment. She set her challah dough down in the kitchen. Then, she went to her room to play. When she was almost finished building her castle out of magnetic tiles, she stood back to look at it.

"You'll be my new home," she said, "if only I was smaller or you were bigger."

Thump. Thump.

What was that? Raizy looked around. The thumping stopped. Maybe it was just her imagination. She went back to finishing her castle.

Thump. Thump. Thump. Thump.

Okay, now there was no denying it. Something was definitely making that sound. Maybe it was the other girls. Were they fighting again?

Thump.

She looked up from her castle. That's weird. It sounded as if it was inside the apartment. Raizy looked toward the vent in the corner of her room. She got up and walked toward it.

Thump.

Was it coming from there? She put her ear to the vent. The thumps appeared to stop and then ...

Oh no.

Lots of challah dough streamed out of the vent.

At Atara's, Atara was busy practicing her dance routine. Then, a loud, THUMP - THUMP – THUMP, mixed up the beat. This caused her to mix up her dance moves. She turned off the music.

Thump.

Strange. She put her ear to her phone. Maybe it was coming from there. Nope.

Thump. Thump. Thump.

Maybe it was Raizy playing her horrible music. She would tell her to stop. Atara felt a tap on her back. She turned around and then …

Oh no. Standing there was a giant Challah Monster looking her in the face. It gushed toward her.

"Blahhhhhhhhhh!"

Atara screamed.

In her room, Maya was busy reading when she heard a thumping coming from somewhere.

Thump.

She assumed it was Sheva who sometimes banged on the wall to annoy her.

Thump. Thump.

She put down her book.

Thump. Thump. Thump.

She got up and opened the door and then ...

Oh No.

Maya slipped on the river of challah rushing down her hallway.

At Sheva's, Sheva was busy boxing. She punched the punching bag a few times. Then, she took a break.

Thump. Thump.

She looked down at her boxing gloves.

Thump. Thump. Thump.

The ceiling shook. That definitely wasn't her.

Thump. Thump. Thump. Thump.

For sure it was Atara practicing her dance routine. She would go up and yell at her. She stormed across the room and then ...

Oh no.

Challah poured down on Sheva in a ginormous challah shower.

Raizy rushed to the kitchen where she had set down the challah dough to rise. She shrieked. Her kitchen was completely filled with dough.

The girls rushed out of their apartments. They collided.

"Watch where you're going," yelled each girl. They looked at each other. Then Maya who never spoke, spoke.

"Why are we all covered in challah?"

*
*   *
*   *

2

Challah Denial

None of the girls wanted to admit that their challah dough was to blame.

"Well I just thought it would be good for my hair," said Atara.

Sheva who was completely covered in dough answered, "And I, I, I... just thought challah would be good for my hair and skin."

Raizy looked down at her shirt which was completely covered in dough.

"Well I wanted to see if could make a shirt out of challah," chimed Raizy.

THE CHALLAH THAT TOOK OVER THE HOUSE

"That's a silly idea," shouted the other girls.

"Really?" Raizy looked at them. "Is it any sillier than bathing in challah or using it as gel?"

"Hey!" Sheva said. "Maya never answered." She looked at Maya. "Why are you covered in dough?"

Maya looked down. She was shy. People giving her so much attention, made her turn bright red.

"It's her," yelled Sheva. "It's her fault we're all covered in dough." They all glared at Maya.

"Just a second ago, you guys said you were using it for your hair and skin," stammered Maya.

"I lied," admitted Sheva.

"Me too," admitted Atara and Raizy.

"Challah has taken over my apartment," said Sheva.

"Mine too," responded Atara and Raizy.

"It's because of her. I know it," yelled Sheva, pointing at Maya.

Everyone circled Maya.

"That's impossible," responded Maya. "In my place, challah was dripping from the ceiling which means it must be one of you."

Each girl glanced around deciding who to blame next. Then, they all fought and blamed each other.

"Stop it," yelled Raizy. "Who cares whose fault it is? We have only a short time before our parents get home. Unless we deal with this mess, there will be no Shabbos for any of us."

"She's right," said a voice.

They all turned around.

"Over here," said the voice.

They looked toward the stairs. On the top was challah dough. The dough looked to be a blend of each girl's challah. It was spicy, sweet, saucy and chocolaty. It formed a mouth and spoke to them.

"I've taken over your home because you girls were mean to each other and now I won't give it back.

The challah dough began to roll full speed down the stairs toward them.

"Run," yelled Raizy.

The girls ran and took cover outside. The Challah Monster slammed the door behind them.

"Oh no," exclaimed the girls.

"What are we going to do?" cried Sheva.

3

Challah Tactics

"We could pray," suggested Maya.

"We could," agreed Raizy.

"Yeah right. Nothing short of magic will make that blob of dough disappear," said Sheva.

Atara chirped in. "What if we tied a giant red string around it to ward of the evil eye?"

Sheva laughed. "Or we could build a giant challah golden calf and worship it too."

"I'm going to pray," insisted Maya.

Atara was doubtful. "As if that's going to work."

Sheva agreed. "There's a time to pray and a time to act."

Maya thought to herself, what do the other girls know? Praying never failed her before. With her book of prayers by King David in hand, Maya tiptoed up to the door.

Sheva yelled after her, "When our people left Egypt, Nahson took that step into the sea. He didn't just pray, you know? Neither did King David."

Maya stood at the door. She opened her prayer book. At that moment, a big clump of dough oozed out of the window.

"Watch out," yelled Sheva but it was too late.

The big clump of dough landed on Maya's head.

Splat.

Maya walked back to the group with dough in her hair. Atara giggled.

Surprised, Maya looked at Sheva. "You warned me?"

"Tried," corrected Sheva.

"Thanks," said Maya.

"You should have listened to me though, there's a time to pray-"

"And a time to act," interrupted Atara. "Sheva, if you're so brave, why don't you go and beat it up?"

4

Challah Punches

"Right, like she's going to beat up the Challah Monster. It's three thousand times her size," exclaimed Raizy.

Maya piped in, "Well we're all scared of her, so why wouldn't Mr. Challah Monster be scared as well?"

"Good point," agreed the other girls.

"You guys are scared of me?" Sheva laughed. She stormed up to the front door. "I'll punch the Nebakanezer out of that thing."

She opened the door and gave the challah a beating. By the end, she was sweating.

Unfortunately, all her effort barely produced a dent. The Challah Monster laughed and slammed the door. Sheva backed up.

"Watch out," yelled Maya.

Sheva had almost backed into the challah dough on the ground. If Maya hadn't warned her, Sheva would have slipped.

"Thanks," Sheva said to Maya, "but looks like that didn't work." Sheva shrugged her shoulders.

"We're never going to defeat it, it's too big." Atara pouted.

Raizy looked to the spot where the dough had fallen. Suddenly, the dough shrank to half its size.

"Guys, look!" Raizy pointed to the dough. "It shrunk."

"Maybe it was the prayers?" suggested Maya.

"Or maybe it shrunk because you guys helped each other along with praying," piped Raizy.

"That's ridiculous," exclaimed Sheva. "You're saying by only being nice to each other that all of this." Sheva pointed at the house overflowing with dough. "Will magically disappear?"

"Maybe," answered Raizy, suddenly unsure. Raizy's fear spread to the other girls. The challah must have sensed their fear because it started to expand and expand.

Raizy watched the challah pour out of the window on to the grass. It was moving even faster. If they didn't do something soon, it could take over the whole block. The more fear they showed, the faster the challah poured out.

"It's feeding on our fear," yelled Raizy.

"We have to stop being afraid," yelled Atara.

"I can't," cried Maya. "I'm scared."

"You guys are wimps," yelled Sheva. "If we're going to do something we need to do it now."

"What if instead of fighting it, we helped it?" piped Raizy.

The girls looked at Raizy as if she was crazy. There was now a giant, expanding, challah puddle on the grass, under her window.

"Help it?" yelled Sheva. "You mean help it take over the whole block?"

"No guys. Listen. We help it by baking it." Raizy pointed to the house. "If we bake the outside, it may stop it from growing or at the least, buy us time."

"And how do we do that?" Sheva asked, "got a gigantic stove?"

"No." Raizy sulked.

"But we could surround it with tin foil," suggested Atara. "That way the sun will bake it."

"And where do we find tin foil?" asked Sheva.

"I know! In the basement storage room, my mom stores a lot in bulk," exclaimed Atara.

They looked toward the basement. Challah oozed out of the windows.

5

Challah move!

"It's in the back room," said Atara. "Maybe the Challah didn't get in there."

"And how do we get in there?" Raizy asked.

Sheva ran to the side of the house and produced two shovels and two yogurt containers. "We can take turns."

They began shoveling. It wasn't working so well. As they shoveled, the challah would just fill up any space made. They sat on the ground, ready to give up.

"I know." Atara got up. She returned with a long play tunnel from the back yard. She stuck the tunnel into the dough. Everyone helped shovel out the center.

Finally, they had created a tunnel that could be crawled through. They could see the handle of the backroom door. Atara crawled through. She got to the door handle and turned.

The girls sighed in relief. The room was free of challah. Atara threw boxes of tin foil out. Sheva and Raizy caught them. Maya counted the boxes. They had ten. With the foil, they covered the entire house.

"Guys look!" Raizy pointed. The challah had stopped expanding. She lifted the tin foil and looked underneath. The challah was baked.

Atara high fived Raizy. "Good job"

Raizy smiled. "We did it."

The challah had stopped growing and it appeared to have receded a bit.

"But guys," said Maya, "our house is still filled with bread."

Maya was right. The girls had temporarily stopped the Challah Monster, but who knew how long that would last? The inside was probably not fully baked. For all they knew, the dough could start rising again, even more rapidly.

6

Challah, help!

"We could eat it," suggested Atara who was now hungry after all the exercise.

"Hey, she's on to something," piped Sheva. "Raizy said that the Challah Monster likes when we work together. Well what if we had a neighborhood bake sale and shared our bread with the block?"

"I like that idea," said Raizy.

"Me too," responded the other girls.

Raizy helped Atara set up the tables and Maya was in charge of cash. Sheva publicized the event and invited all her friends. So did the other girls. Soon enough there was a crowd outside. The girls had worked extra hard to create one hundred loaves of dough to sell. Now, the hallway entrance was completely cleared out.

However, after awhile people stopped buying challah. They just socialized on the lawn and played games.

"What do we do? We've only cleared out the front hall. There's still a house full of challah," Atara exclaimed. She looked at Raizy. Raizy had to get creative. She stood on a platform.

"Guys, we're having a contest. Whoever creates the most interesting thing to make out of challah wins."

"Wins what?" a boy in the crowd asked.

"Wins a … a …." Raizy stammered.

Atara chimed in, "A vacation."

"Passover in Israel," shouted Sheva and Maya, together.

"Our house is filled with challah so grab as much as you want. Make whatever you want. Be creative and you might win Passover in Israel," Atara beamed.

Everyone on the lawn rushed into the house and began removing challah dough.

Raizy said to Atara, "Why did we promise them that? How are we going to give anyone a vacation?"

At that moment, the news crew that Atara called showed up. "You called reporters?" exclaimed Maya.

A blond reporter from Channel 6 stood in front of their house. "In a publicity stunt, a group of girls are offering a free Passover vacation to Israel to whoever removes the most dough."

The reporter pointed the microphone at Raizy. "What a great idea to completely fill your house with bread. Was that your idea?"

"It was ours," answered Raizy. A nervous laugh escaped Maya's mouth. The other girls half smiled.

"It's a pre-Pesach chametz party," piped in Sheva.

"Yay," exclaimed Atara.

Challah cakes, challah bracelets, challah necklaces and challah dolls were made.

Raizy held up a challah in the shape of a t-shirt.

"Nice," said Sheva.

It was time for the girls to choose a winner. Raizy pulled the girls aside. "What are we going to do? We lied. We can't give anyone a vacation."

A little boy overheard. He yelled to everyone, "The girls are liars! There is no contest! There is no trip to Israel!"

The crowd was angry. They threw their challah dough at the girls. The Challah Monster learned of what happened and he was not happy. He got angrier and angrier and angrier.

The Challah Monster bellowed, "You people are the worst. You don't get along and now I'm going to take over your whole block." Then, he poured out of the house at rapid speed.

"Blahhhhh."

There was chaos. The crowd ran in every direction. Raizy and her friends took cover in the treehouse.

"What are we going to do?" asked Atara.

7

Challah Flood

"We could run," suggested Maya.

"No running," yelled Sheva, "we're not cowards. The neighborhood is relying on us."

"She's right," said Raizy.

"It's our mess, we have to clean it up," agreed Atara.

"So what do we do?" asked Raizy. "Come on think."

"Well, we were wrong to lie to everyone about a prize. So, what if we made it right by doing the steps to forgiveness that I learned in torah class?" suggested Maya.

"Which are?" asked Sheva.

"Recognizing you did wrong, saying you won't do it again, and giving to charity," piped Raizy.

Atara looked at the house and the lawn covered with dough. "We were so wrong."

"Step One," said Raizy.

"We're so not ever doing this again," said Atara.

"Step Two," said Maya.

"Now what do we do for charity?" asked Raizy.

"Instead of selling the challah-" said Sheva.

"We can give it to a shelter," piped Maya.

"Step Three," said Raizy.

"And how are we going to do that?" asked Atara.

"There's a shelter five blocks away," said Sheva. "My brother sometimes volunteers there."

"Are we adults?" exclaimed Atara. "Can anyone here drive?"

The other girls shook their heads.

"I didn't think so," said Atara.

"My bike," said Sheva. "I can ride my bike."

"Yeah, good luck fitting all that dough on the back of your bicycle," added Atara.

"Well she doesn't have to fit it on the back," said Maya. "She could pull it."

One problem. Sheva remembered that she had lent her bike to her cousin.

"I have a bike," said Raizy. "But it's in my place and it's probably covered in bread. Though, maybe not. It's in the storage closet which doesn't have any vents."

They looked up at Raizy's bedroom window. Challah oozed out.

"Got any idea how to get it?" asked Maya.

"I don't know why we didn't think of this before," chimed Atara, "what if we told the Challah Monster it's Passover?"

"Didn't lying get us into this mess?" asked Raizy.

"And isn't that one of the things we agreed not to do again?" asked Maya.

"Well yeah," said Atara, "but in Egypt, God told Moses to ask Pharaoh to let us have two weeks in the desert. Really we were going to take off after the two weeks."

"But of course, we didn't tell Pharaoh that. We just left out that little part for a higher cause," said Raizy. "Isn't Shabbat a higher cause? We don't even have to lie so much. We could-"

"Passover songs! We could just start singing Passover songs," yelled Sheva.

"Pretend it's already Pesach. Genius. It's not like we're saying it is," yelled Maya.

The girls joined hands and started to sing, "Day, dayeinu."

"Enough of this dough," Sheva exclaimed. "I can't wait not to see bread."

They sang, "Dayeinu." The Challah Monster heard them singing and panicked.

"It's Pesach?" the Challah Monster yelled, "why didn't anyone tell me?" And with that he started to shrink.

Raizy ran through the front door and made it to her room. There she quickly opened the storage closet and pulled out her bike.

The Challah Monster shrunk and shrunk until it saw the calendar that Raizy's mom had stuck to the fridge. The calendar clearly marked the days of Passover.

"What, it's not Pesach?" the Challah Monster yelled and with that it started to expand again. It grew and grew.

Raizy rushed into her bedroom. She slammed the door. The Challah Monster threw open her door and grew and grew.

Soon Raizy was pushed up against the window. She opened it. What could she do? With quick thinking, she began to braid the dough.

Then she threw down her bike. It landed in a pile of leaves. Then, she grabbed the braided challah dough and climbed down. Raizy was almost at the bottom, when the braid broke. She landed in a pile of leaves.

Now to attach it to the bike. The girls grabbed the dough. Together they pulled it toward the bike. Then, they attached it to the end. Sheva cycled off. Unfortunately, only a moment later the challah broke.

8

Challah Trails

"We'll braid it," said Sheva, "like Raizy did."

"A braid is stronger than one strand," said Maya.

"But my braid broke," said Raizy.

"It did," responded Sheva, "but what if we used four strands instead of three?"

"A fishtail braid?" asked Atara who had just learned to do them.

"With four strands, it will be even harder than three to break," said Sheva.

They divided the bread into four strands, one representing each one of them. They each took a strand and pulled it out as far as they could, to the end of their lawn. Then, they braided the dough.

Then, Sheva got on her bike. She tried one more time to pull the challah dough out of her house. This time it worked. Challah flowed out the front door.

The Challah Monster saw the girls working together and not giving up. He grew less angry and his heart warmed. His heart warmed so much that even part of the challah dough that wasn't braided, braided itself.

A giant braided challah trailed from the back of the bike. A kid on the street did a double take. So did a rabbi who was returning from shul. The other girls ran beside Sheva as she bicycled.

Sheva pulled up to the homeless shelter. "Now what?" asked Sheva.

They had made it to the shelter but there was still a giant trail of dough behind her. She got off the bike.

"I know," said Maya. She got on the bike. The other girls watched as she rode around and around in a circle. As she did so, the challah formed a mountain.

When the last bit of challah was added to the mountain, they walked up to the door of the shelter and rang the bell.

Maya pulled on Raizy's shirt.

Raizy swung around. "What?"

"Isn't the best mitzvah done without taking credit?" said Maya.

"She's right," said Atara. "We can do a good deed without letting everyone know it's us."

"Oh come on," said Raizy, "with all our hard work, I want to see their faces." Raizy looked at Sheva.

"I'm with them. We can still see their reaction from afar," said Sheva.

"Oh fine," said Raizy, "maybe you're right."

The girls pulled Raizy away and they watched from a hiding place the excited reactions of the homeless people and the staff.

9

Challah Clean Up

The girls returned home. Their parents would be back any second. While the challah was gone, their apartments were an absolute mess. There were tons of crumbs. Cleaning up for Passover would be a nightmare.

The girls walked back outside. There was no way they would ever clean it up in time. Feeling the situation was hopeless, they sat down in the outdoor tree house. Their lawn was completely overturned. Chairs were scattered about and tables flipped over. It looked as if their house had been hit by a hurricane.

"Our parents are going to kill us," said Sheva.

Maya laughed. "I didn't think you were scared of anything."

"I act tough," said Sheva. "I'm Israeli. We must be or the world walks all over us. You know, after today, I think you're pretty tough too."

Maya picked up the vase. Inside was all the money they had earned at the bake sale.

"Wow guys, look," exclaimed Maya. The vase was filled with cash.

"Looks like we can send a winner to Israel after all," exclaimed Atara.

"They really liked our challah," shouted Raizy.

Sheva decided that she would taste Maya's challah. She took some off the slide.

"It's sweet, I like it," said Sheva.

Maya decided that she would taste Sheva's dough. She took some off the swing.

"This challah is spicy," said Maya. "I like it."

Raizy tasted some of Atara's challah off the monkey bars. "I never thought I'd like pizza in challah."

Atara tasted some of Raizy's challah off the rope ladder. "Oooh chocolaty."

Maya grabbed it and took a bite. "Wow! Chocolate does go well in challah after all."

Sheva stood up. "Guys, look."

They looked toward their house. Their good behavior must have been seen and their prayers must have been heard because everything had returned to normal. There were no crumbs at all anywhere.

Their parents returned home. They didn't notice anything out of order and nobody got in trouble. That Shabbat, all of the girls were nice to each other and played with each other and finally took a much deserved Shabbos snooze.

10

Challah Recipe

Ingredients for Dough:

2 ½ cups warm water
2 ¼ tsp. active dry yeast
½ cup sugar
2 eggs plus 1 egg for glaze
1 tbsp. Salt
¼ cup oil plus some to oil the tin
8 – 9 cups unbleached flour or light spelt flour
Note: This recipe makes 4 challahs

Additional Ingredients for Personalization:

Raizy's Chocolate Chip Challah:

2 cups of chocolate chips

Chocolate Drizzle (optional - recipe on last step)

Atara's Pizza Challah:

1 can of tomato sauce

2 cloves of Garlic

3-4 tbsp. of olive oil

Handful of Shredded Mozzarella or Vegan Mozzarella (optional)

Maya's Cinnamon Bun Challah:

For Dusting: 2-3 tbsp. of sugar & cinnamon

Top Crumble: a couple of spoonsful of flour mixed with sugar and a pinch of cinnamon with a few drops of oil.

2 cup Raisins

Vegan Icing (optional - recipe on last step)

Sheva's Golden Challah:

8 tbsp. of turmeric

Sesame and /or poppy seeds to sprinkle on top

Directions:

1.Place lukewarm water into a large bowl. Sprinkle in yeast. Let stand for 5 minutes.

2.Add the sugar, eggs, salt, oil and beat with wire whisk for several minutes.

3. Add flour 1 cup at a time while stirring. After ½ of the total flour has been added, kneed in the rest using a machine with a dough hook.

<u>For Sheva's Golden Challah:</u> Add turmeric and kneed with the machine.

4. Even if the dough is still sticky, scrape it out of the bowl onto a floured surface & roll into a ball.

5. Place dough into a large oiled bowl. Roll it around to coat it with the oil. Cover and place in fridge overnight or for at least 8 hours. When removed let rise for 1 hour.

6. Punch down the dough. Return to floured surface and divide into 4 equal sized balls for 4 loaves of challah.

7. <u>For Raizy's Chocolate Challah:</u>
Work 1/4 -2/4 cup of choc. chips into each ball.

For Maya's Cinnamon Bun Challah:

Work in 1/4 to 2/4 cup of raisins into each ball.

8. For Atara's Pizza Challah:

Stretch out the dough of each ball. Brush lightly with tomato sauce & sprinkle mozzarella. (Repeat with rest of dough for 3 more loaves or save for later.)

For Maya's Cinnamon Bun Challah:

Stretch out the dough like a pizza, dust with cinnamon mixed with a little sugar. (Repeat with rest of dough for 3 more loaves or save for later.)

9. For Raizy's Chocolate Challah & Sheva's Golden Challah & Maya's Cinnamon Challah

Make a long rope with each ball and follow the instructions for the 5-strand braid (next page).

For Atara's Pizza Challah:

Do not make rope or braid (skip next step). Roll up like a jelly roll and cut into five pieces (four pieces are symbolic of the character of each of the girls + the fifth is symbolic of you). We all work together to make Judaism great!

*
  *
*   *

5-Strand Braid

Each of the four stands represents one of the girls in this story. The 5th strand represents You! J We all go together to make Judaism great.

Step1: For each ball of challah, divide into 5 equal strands & separate 2 strands on the left side, three strands on the right.

Step 2: Bring the outermost strand on the right side (Strand E) across to the left side.

Step 3: Bring the outermost strand on the left side (Strand A) across to the right side so that Strand E and Strand A form an X in the center.

Step 4: Repeat – Now bring Strand D across from the right side to the left side.

Step 5: Bring Strand B across to the right side.

Step 6: Repeat until completely braided.

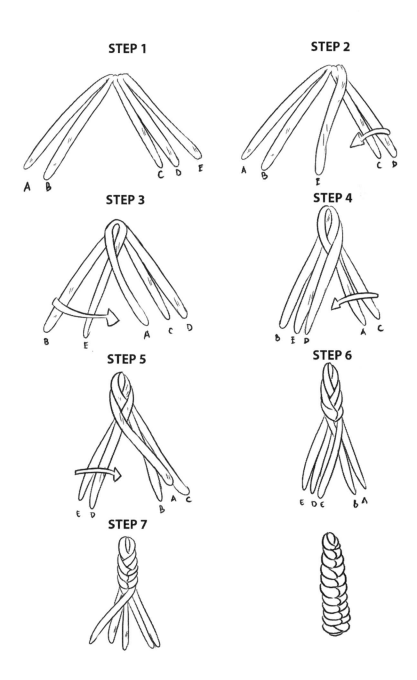

STEP 1

STEP 2

STEP 3

STEP 4

STEP 5

STEP 6

STEP 7

Directions (Continued):

10.   Preheat Oven to 350ºF regular oven 325ºF convection.

11.   <u>For Raizy's Chocolate Challah, Maya's Cinnamon Bun Challah, Sheva's Golden Challah:</u> Place braids in parchment paper lined loaf pans, oiled brioche tins or on a baking sheet. Cover with tea towel and let rise again for 45 minutes.

<u>For Atara's Pizza Challah:</u>

Place in 6" round pan brushed with crushed garlic in oil (leave some to brush on challah). Arrange by placing side by side (joining) in a circle with one piece in the center.

12.   Beat remaining egg, and brush it onto the risen loaves for all challahs.

13.   <u>For Atara's Pizza Challah:</u>

Brush any of the remaining garlic oil on top.

<u>For Sheva's Golden Challah:</u> Top with white & black sesame seeds.

<u>For Maya's Cinnamon Bun Challah</u>
Sprinkle on top flour-sugar mixed 1:1. Add a pinch of cinnamon, moistened with oil and mixed until crumbly.

14.   Baking Times:
<u>Raizy's Chocolate Challah, Maya's Cinnamon Bun Challah & Sheva's Golden Challah:</u>
Bake 23-24 minutes
<u>Atara's Pizza Challah</u>
Bake 28 minutes

15.   Bake for appropriate time or until the breads give off a hollow sound when thumped on the bottom. Remove from pan and cool on rack.

16.   After Additions (optional):
<u>For Razi's Challah:</u> Melt white + dark chocolate chips and drizzle on top. (place in fridge afterwards to harden)
<u>For Atara's Pizza Challah:</u> Place tomato sauce in small bowls for dipping.
<u>For Sheva's Golden Challah:</u> Serve with spicy hummus.

<u>For Maya's Cinnamon Bun Challah:</u>
For vegan icing mix:
1 cup vegan butter
2 cups confectioners sugar
1 tbsp + 2 tsp. vegan milk
¾ tsp. apple cider vinegar
1/8 tsp. of salt
¾ tsp. vanilla extract
(chill frosting briefly to optimize the texture)
Drizzle vegan icing on top of challah.

Your
Challah Toppings

What would you add to your challah to make it yours? Honey drizzle? Caramel drizzle? Chocolate sprinkles?

My Challah Toppings:

*
*   *

ABOUT THE AUTHOR

Melissa Berg is the author of the popular haggadah, "Pop Haggadah," that was featured in The Jewish Journal of Los Angeles, The Baltimore Jewish Times, The Washington Jewish Week and The Huffington Post.

ALSO AVAILABLE FROM
ECLECTIC IVRI PRESS: